Chimpanzees for TEA!

by

Jo Empson

PUFFIN

"Hey, Vincent!
This cupboard is looking a bit bare.
Can you rush to the shops . . .

. . . and get:

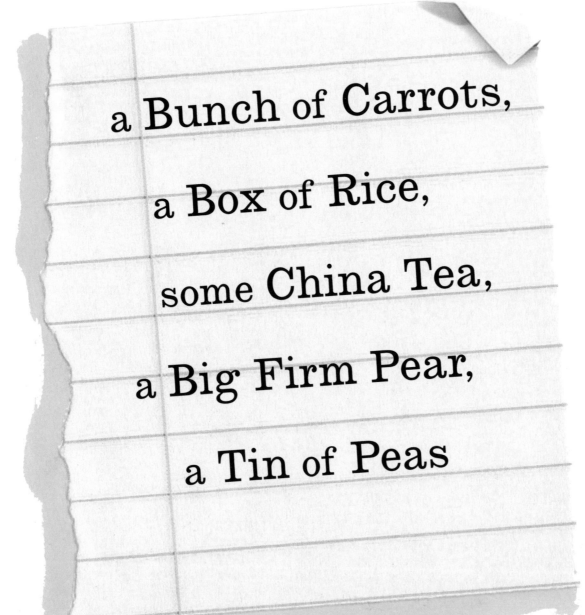

a Bunch of Carrots,

a Box of Rice,

some China Tea,

a Big Firm Pear,

a Tin of Peas

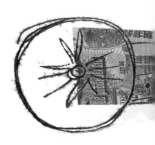

and hurry home in time for tea!"

Sorry, can't stop, Mr Singh.
I've got to rush to the shops and get . . .
a Bunch of Carrots, a Box of Rice,
some China Tea, a Big Firm Pear, a Tin of Peas

and hurry home in time for tea.   BUT . . .

Oh

NO...

the

list!

What was it? Umm . . . a Bunch of Carrots . . . errr . .

Box of Rice, some China Tea . . . . a Big Firm Pear . . .

...a Trapeze and hurry home in time for tea.

... I've got to rush to the shops and get a Bunc.

f Carrots, a Box of Rice, some China Tea . . . .

aaaa . . .

aaaa . . .

aaaand . . .

. . . a Big Furry Bear, a Trapeze

and hurry hom

n time for tea.

Hey, Vincent . . .

ZOO

Sorry, can't stop, Mr Wood.
I've got to rush to the shops
and get . . .

a Bunch of Carrots,
a Box of Rice . . .

. . . some Chimpanzees, a Big Furry

Bear, a Trapeze . . .

and hurry home
in time for tea.

ush to the shops and get a Bunch of Carrots . . .

Pet Shop

Hire a Hat

...a **Box of Mice**, some Chimpanzees,
a Big Furry Bear, a Trapeze
and hurry home in time for tea.

Ahh, Vincent . . .

Sorry, can't stop, Mrs Rae.
I've got to rush to the shops
and get . . .

. . . a Branch of Parrots,
a Box of Mice, some Chimpanzees,

a Big Furry Bear, a Trapeze. Hurry home

and . . .

. . . invit

hem ALL in for . . .

..tea!

For John with love and thanks.

PUFFIN BOOKS
UK | USA | Canada | Ireland | Australia | India | New Zealand | South Africa
Puffin Books is part of the Penguin Random House group of companies
whose addresses can be found at global.penguinrandomhouse.com.
puffinbooks.com
First published 2016
001
Text and illustrations copyright © Jo Empson, 2016
The moral right of the author/illustrator has been asserted
Printed in China
ISBN: 978–0–141–35643–3